Mrs. Crump's Cat

by Linda Smith

pictures by David Roberts

HarperCollins Publishers

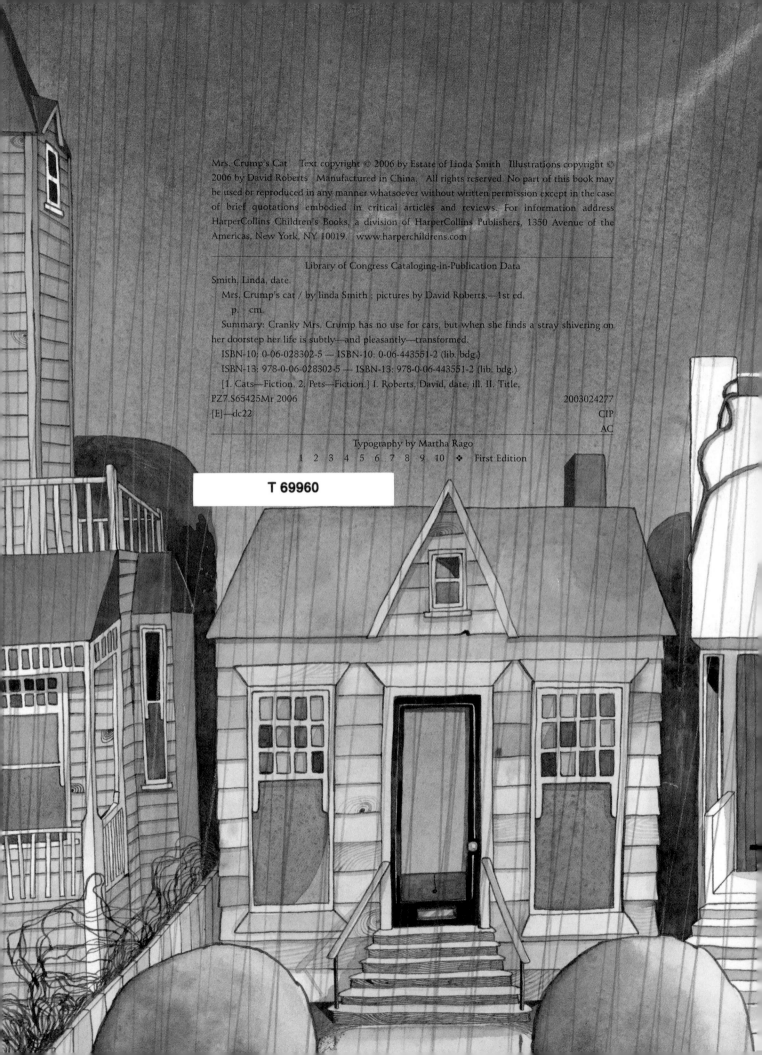

Library of Congress Cataloging-in-Publication Data

Smith, Linda, date.

Mrs. Crump's cat / by linda Smith ; pictures by David Roberts.—1st ed.

p.   cm.

Summary: Cranky Mrs. Crump has no use for cats, but when she finds a stray shivering on her doorstep her life is subtly—and pleasantly—transformed.

ISBN-10: 0-06-028302-5 — ISBN-10: 0-06-443551-2 (lib. bdg.)

ISBN-13: 978-0-06-028302-5 — ISBN-13: 978-0-06-443551-2 (lib. bdg.)

[1. Cats—Fiction. 2. Pets—Fiction.] I. Roberts, David, date, ill. II. Title.

PZ7.S65425Mr 2006   2003024277

[E]—dc22   CIP
                                                                                        AC

Typography by Martha Rago

1 2 3 4 5 6 7 8 9 10 ❖ First Edition

Dedicated to Janie Bynum and
Katie Davis,
for their beautiful friendship,
encouragement, and guidance.
—L.S.

For Louisa and her menagerie
of waifs and strays
—D.R.

ONE RAINY DAY Mrs. Crump opened her front door to fetch the paper and discovered an exquisite golden cat shivering on her porch step.

"Shoo!" she cried. "Shoo! Go away!"

But the cat did not go away.

"I'll have you know," Mrs. Crump said, "I have no use for a cat."

Mrs. Crump turned away, but somehow the door did
not quite shut . . . and the cat slipped in.

"I should have known," Mrs. Crump said. "Cats are
sneaky by nature."

She wrestled a log into place, then watched as the cat preened and primped and polished itself in front of the fire.

When the cat is dry, Mrs. Crump thought, I'll send it on its way.

But when the cat was dry, it curled itself around Mrs. Crump's ankles like a soft velvet ribbon and mewed hungrily.

Mrs. Crump went to her pantry and got a slice of bread, but the cat would not go near it.

  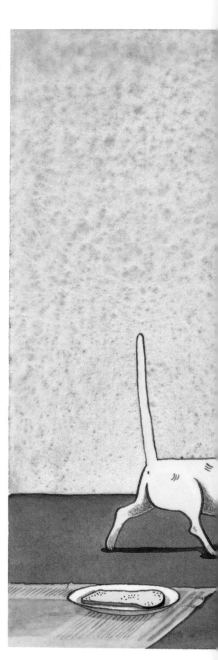

"Just as I suspected," Mrs. Crump said. "Cats are finicky as well."

Mrs. Crump decided she would have
to go to town, and she threw on her
overcoat.

"Tonight," she said to the cat, "I'll
send you on your way."

Mr. Henry nodded his head and said, "Good day!" when Mrs. Crump entered his store.

"Good day to you," she said curtly, and was a bit surprised she'd said even that. Mrs. Crump paid for a pint of cream and had started on her way when she changed her mind.

"What is it? Something else?" the grocer asked.

And before she even thought the words, Mrs. Crump found herself asking that a shiny red pet dish be added to her order.

"Do you have a new dog?" Mr. Henry asked.

"I do not," Mrs. Crump said. "I have a stray cat."

"Don't feed it," Mr. Henry warned. "If you do, you'll never be rid of it."

It was the strangest thing, Mrs. Crump thought, but somehow the way back home seemed far shorter than the way there.

That night Mrs. Crump filled the shiny red dish with cream and added another log to the fire. Soon the bowl was empty and the cat was full.

It was time to put the cat out.

Mrs. Crump stood at the door with the cat in her arms. She looked up at the clear, starry sky. She poked her nose out and sniffed the cool, dry air. Mrs. Crump looked down at the cat. The cat looked up and purred magnificently.

"I smell rain," Mrs. Crump decided, slamming the door shut. It would be foolish to turn out a dry cat only to have a wet one on the porch step again come morning.

"Tomorrow," she said to the cat, "I will
send you on your way."

The next day was bright and sunny, and Mrs. Crump was a bit disappointed. It was a lovely day to turn the cat out. But it seemed such a shame to waste a half pint of cream when she had traveled so far to buy it.

"It will only spoil," Mrs. Crump decided. "When the cream is gone, I'll send the cat on its way."

Mrs. Crump poured the last of the cream at breakfast.

The cat stretched and yawned and circled the bowl, then stopped . . .

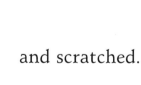

and scratched.

Mrs. Crump parted a bit of its golden fur and saw, to her horror, a single flea flitting between the cat's ears.

"I will not have critters of that sort in my house," Mrs. Crump declared.

"Before you go anywhere," she said to the cat, "you'll need a good scrubbing with brown soap.

"A lot of trouble you are," Mrs. Crump said, throwing on her overcoat. She pulled the door shut behind her and headed for town.

"Hello again," Mr. Henry said as Mrs. Crump entered his store.

"And hello again to you," she said, but not quite as curtly
as before.

Mrs. Crump paid for a bar of brown soap and a pint of cream,
and had started on her way when she changed her mind.

"What is it? Something else?" the grocer asked. And before she even thought the words, Mrs. Crump found herself asking that a dainty yellow collar with a silver bell be added to the order.

"I take it you still have the cat," Mr. Henry said.

"I would have turned that cat out long ago," Mrs. Crump explained, "but it's been one thing after another. And now I'm afraid the cat has forgotten its way."

"Hang a sign in my store," Mr. Henry suggested. "If someone claims the cat, your troubles will be over!"

"And if no one claims the cat?" Mrs. Crump asked.

"I'm afraid you'll have no choice but to keep it," Mr. Henry admitted.

It was the strangest thing, but somehow Mrs. Crump had never noticed before what a smart man Mr. Henry was.

That evening, after the cat's bath, Mrs. Crump made up a sign. A very small sign.

She started to write, "FOUND. One exquisite golden cat. Inquire within."

But she changed her mind. She turned the paper over and thought a bit.

"I did not find *you*," she said to the cat. "You were on *my* porch step, after all."

She wrote the word "Found" in very small letters.

"You've been sneaky and finicky and plenty of trouble," Mrs. Crump reminded the cat.

"And you were not really very exquisite when you found me," Mrs. Crump decided. "You were wet."

Mrs. Crump wrote the word "**WET**" in very large letters.

"I could hardly have called you golden," Mrs. Crump said. "You looked plain yellow to me."

Mrs. Crump wrote "yellow" next to the word "**WET**."

And to be fair, Mrs. Crump thought, I mustn't forget about the fleas.

Finally, she set the sign down and stood back to admire her work.

It read:

Found
one sneaky
finicky
troublesome
WET yellow cat
with FLEAS

Mrs. Crump was at Mr. Henry's store first thing in the morning. She pinned the sign in a dusty corner, and Mr. Henry promised to let her know the minute someone inquired about the cat.

The very next evening, in fact, Mrs. Crump
was back at Mr. Henry's store.

"Sorry," Mr. Henry said. "No one asked about
the cat today."

"A pity," Mrs. Crump said, paying for six fat
livers and a can of tuna.

Mrs. Crump found herself singing on
the way home.

Finally, at the end of the week, Mr. Henry showed up at Mrs. Crump's door with the dusty sign in his hands. No one had claimed the

sneaky,

finicky,

troublesome,

wet,

yellow cat with fleas.

It was the strangest thing, but somehow Mrs. Crump was not the least bit surprised.

"It's just as well," Mr. Henry said. "You have bought a collar, soap, livers, tuna, two full pints of cream, and a shiny red dish. You may as well have a cat to go with them."

"Now, how could this happen?" Mrs. Crump wondered. "I had no use for a cat."

"Cats are clever that way," Mr. Henry said. "Before you know it, you'll be sitting by the fire with the cat on your lap, wondering how you ever got along without it."

That night Mrs. Crump
put an extra log on the fire
and did just that.

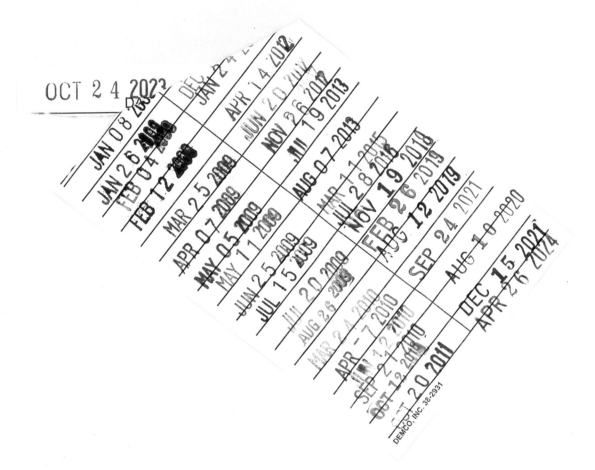
PORTLAND DISTRICT LIBRARY
334 Kent St.
PORTLAND, MI 48875